Tugboat Tank

PAGE PUBLISHING, INC.
New York, NY

First originally published by Page Publishing, Inc. 2019

ISBN 978-1-64350-250-2 (Paperback)
ISBN 978-1-64350-252-6 (Hardcover)
ISBN 978-1-64350-251-9 (Digital)

Printed in the United States of America

Tugboat Tank

by Jamie Hughes

I dedicate this book to my wonderful children,
Madelyn, Lloyd and William.
You inspire me.

There once was a tugboat named Tank. He was red and blue and very strong. Tank had an important job to do. He was responsible for the safety of all of the boats in Happy Harbor Marina.

One day, a large storm was moving in. Tank looked around the marina and noticed that three of his friends Maddie, Connor, and Olivia, were not safely docked in the marina. He knew he had to find them before the storm struck, so he started to look.

As he was looking, the winds started to pick up, the waves grew larger, and the sky turned a dark, angry gray. Then the rain started to fall. Tank knew he had limited time to save his friends and help them get back to the marina. He got right to work!

He took out his blue binoculars and searched the horizon. Far off, he saw his friend Maddie.

Maddie was a sailboat. She had large pink and white sails and no motor. She had been out on a relaxing boat ride when the storm started to pick up. Before she could react, the wind had knocked down her sail, and she knew she was in trouble!

Tank called out to Maddie saying, "Maddie, Maddie, do you need help?"

Maddie said in a thankful voice, "Yes Tank, I sure do!"

Tank was on the move... "Chug a chug a chug a chug." He sounded like a train chugging his way out of the marina and into the vast sea to help his friend. When he arrived, he moved quickly to connect with Maddie, towing her safely home.

Time was not on his side and the storm was getting worse. Now Tank had to find his other two friends.

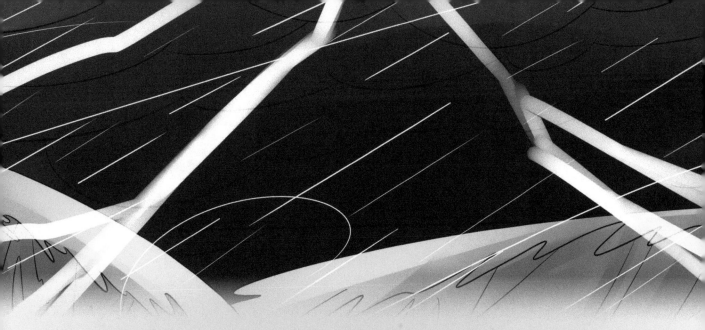

He looked out again and on the horizon he saw his friend Connor. Connor was a big red speed boat, and he liked to race across the water. However, the waves had become so large that they were crashing over the top of his boat and damaged his motor. He knew he was in trouble!

Tank called out to Connor. "Connor, Connor, do you need help?" Connor called back, "Yes, Tank, I sure do!"

Tank was on the move again... "Chug a chug a chug a chug." He again sounded like a train chugging his way out of the marina. When he arrived, he moved quickly to connect with Connor, towing him safely home.

Tank was still missing a friend but the storm had become really dangerous at this point. It was almost too risky for him to leave Happy Harbor Marina, but he knew he couldn't leave his friend behind. So once again, he took out his blue binoculars and looked out on the horizon. Far off, he saw his friend Olivia.

Olivia was a fearsome boat. She had a motor, sails, and never got into trouble. She thought this storm would pass and that she could handle the growing waves, wind, and rain; but she was wrong. Wind and lightning had destroyed her sails, and water crashing over the top of the boat had damaged her engine. She was struck hard and she knew she was in trouble!

There was only one person who could save her now, and he knew what he had to do! Tank called out to Olivia,

"Olivia, Olivia, do you need help?" Olivia called back "Yes Tank, I sure do."

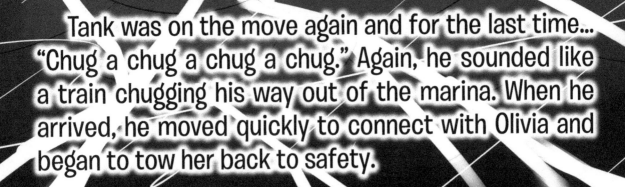

Tank was on the move again and for the last time...
"Chug a chug a chug a chug." Again, he sounded like
a train chugging his way out of the marina. When he
arrived, he moved quickly to connect with Olivia and
began to tow her back to safety.

As he was towing her, the waves got larger and the
rain became stronger. Would he be able to make it
back? Would he be able to save the day?

He began to question himself but he knew deep down he had to save his friend so he pushed on through. He pulled her through the rain, he battled the wind, and he drove through the waves, until he made it through the impossible! He had done it! He finally made it safely back to the marina, and Olivia was so thankful.

Tank's perseverance and thoughtfulness had saved all three of his friends. He was so tired that after checking on his marina one last time, he decided it was time to go to sleep.

18

Through the night, the other boats worked to repair their damaged parts. When they were finished they decided to plan a party. They wanted to reward their hero.

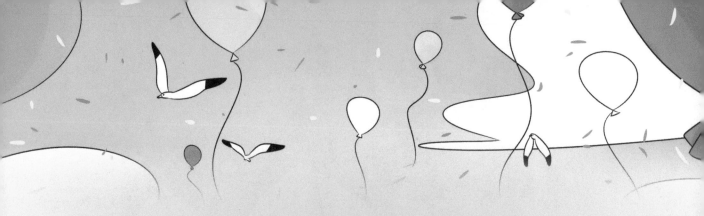

When Tank arose the next morning, all the boats in the marina surrounded him. They began to sing, "Hip hip, hooray! Hip hip, hooray! Thank you, Tank, for saving the day!"

Tank had a smile that lasted for days!

The End.

Tugboat Tank is a story of perseverance. Even when he doubted himself, Tugboat Tank would not give up. When have you persevered? Remember that you can do it and remember to believe in yourself.

About the Author

While writing her stories may be new, Jamie Hughes has been telling stories for years! She is a mother of three children and an avid storyteller! From the moment her daughter Madelyn was old enough to listen, she has been telling her stories at bedtime. Tugboat Tank is just one of those stories. Through the years, the story has changed and has been tweaked (mostly by her kids) until it reached a story that her son Lloyd (aka Tank), her son William, and her daughter Madelyn absolutely love! In fact, they tell each other the story.

Jamie finally decided to put pen to paper and take the story that had brought her family such joy over the years to the world.

She has a clear passion for telling stories, and she is a very animated and positive individual. Her mother always told her to "believe in yourself." She hopes you love this story as much as her family does! If you do, there is more where that came from!